Suki's kimono

With love and thanks to Mom, Dad, Kimi and Maki.
And to Paul, especially. — C.U.

To spunky little kids everywhere. — S.J.

The Japanese words in the story are
geta *(ge-ta)*: Japanese wooden clogs
kimono *(kee-mo-no)*: Japanese robe with wide sleeves
obāchan *(o-baa-chan)*: informal word for grandmother
obi *(o-bee)*: kimono sash
sōmen *(soh-men)*: fine noodle
taiko *(tie-ko)*: Japanese drum

Text © 2003 Chieri Uegaki
Illustrations © 2003 Stéphane Jorisch

Kids Can Press acknowledges the financial support of
the Ontario Arts Council, the Canada Council for the
Arts and the Government of Canada, through the
BPIDP, for our publishing activity.

Published in Canada by
Kids Can Press Ltd.
29 Birch Avenue
Toronto, ON M4V 1E2

Published in the U.S. by
Kids Can Press Ltd.
2250 Military Road
Tonawanda, NY 14150

www.kidscanpress.com

The artwork in this book was rendered in watercolor.
The text is set in Bembo.

Edited by Tara Walker
Designed by Karen Powers
Printed and bound in China

The hardcover edition of this book is smyth
sewn casebound.
The paperback edition of this book is limp sewn with a
drawn-on cover.

CM 03 0 9 8 7 6 5 4
CM PA 05 0 9 8 7 6 5 4 3 2 1

**Library and Archives Canada Cataloguing in
Publication Data**

Uegaki, Chieri
    Suki's kimono / written by Chieri Uegaki ;
illustrated by Stéphane Jorisch.

ISBN 1-55337-084-8 (bound).
ISBN 1-55337-752-4 (pbk.)

I. Jorisch, Stéphane II. Title.

PS8591.E32S83 2003   jC813'.6   C2003-900564-X

Kids Can Press is a *Corus*™ Entertainment company

Suki's Kimono

Written by
CHIERI UEGAKI

Illustrated by
STÉPHANE JORISCH

KIDS CAN PRESS

On the first day of school, Suki wanted to wear her kimono. Her sisters did not approve.

"You can't wear that," said Mari. "People will think you're weird."

"You can't wear that," said Yumi. "Everyone will laugh, and no one will play with you."

"You need something new, Suki."

"You need something cool."

But Suki shook her head. She didn't
care for new. She didn't care for cool.
She wanted to wear her favorite thing.
And her favorite thing was her kimono.

Suki's obāchan had given her the
kimono. The first time Suki wore it, her
obāchan took her to a street festival
where they slurped bowls of slippery,
cold sōmen noodles and shared a cone
of crunchy, shaved ice topped with a
sweet red bean sauce.

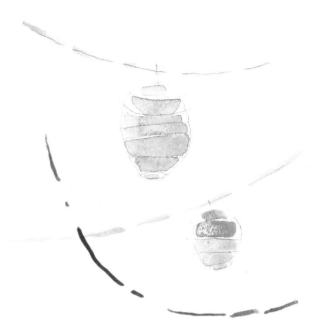

Under strings of paper lanterns, Suki joined her obāchan in a circle dance. She followed her and copied her movements, trying to be as light and as graceful. She watched the other women and children who danced, especially those who were dressed in cotton kimonos like her.

Later, Suki sat so close to the stage that when the taiko drummers performed, *bom-bom-bom-bom*, she felt like she'd swallowed a ball of thunder and her whole insides quaked and quivered.

Before they left the festival, Suki and her obāchan stopped at a souvenir stand. There were many things to choose from, but her obāchan found the prettiest thing of all — a handkerchief of pale pink linen, decorated with tiny maple leaves and cherry blossoms. When she gave it to Suki, she said, "This will help you remember our day."

Now, it was time for school. Mother checked Suki's obi one last time and took a picture of Mari, Yumi and Suki together by the front steps.

Then, as she watched, the three sisters made their way down the block to their school. Mari and Yumi stayed several paces ahead of Suki and pretended they didn't know her.

But Suki didn't mind.

She turned and waved to her mother
before she clip-clopped along in her
shiny red geta, feeling very pleased in her
fan-patterned blue kimono.

Once in a while, Suki would lift her arms and let the butterfly sleeves flutter in the breeze. It made her feel like she'd grown her own set of wings.

When they reached the school, Mari and Yumi hurried across the yard to a group of their friends. Suki stopped and looked around. Some of the children turned and stared at her, and others giggled and pointed at her kimono.

But Suki ignored them.

She took a seat on a swing to wait for the bell. A girl dressed in overalls just like a pair Suki had at home sat on the swing beside her.

"Hi, Suki," said the girl.

"Hi, Penny," said Suki.

"How come you're dressed so funny?"
Penny asked. "Where did you get those shoes?"

Suki lifted her feet off the sand and wiggled her
toes. "I'm not dressed funny," she said. "My grandma gave
me these shoes."

Suki started pumping her legs. After a moment, Penny
did the same, and soon they were both swinging as fast and
as high as they could. *Swoosh, swoosh,* up and up.

When the bell rang, Suki and Penny jumped off their swings and ran to the gym for the first day assembly. Once they were finally taken to their new classroom, Suki chose a desk near the window. Penny chose a desk next to Suki.

As they waited for everyone to find a seat, two boys in front of Suki turned and snickered behind their hands. One of the boys reached over and snatched at Suki's sleeve. "Look at this," he said. "She's a bat!"

Suki felt her cheeks burn, but she did not respond. Instead, she concentrated on sitting up straight and tall, the way her obāchan always did. It was easy to do with an obi wrapped snug around her middle. Her obi was golden yellow, and in its folds Suki had tucked away her pale pink handkerchief.

"Welcome to the first grade," said the teacher. "My name is Mrs. Paggio." She smiled. "Let's introduce ourselves and tell everyone what we did this summer."

When it was her turn to speak, Suki stood up
and told the teacher her name.

"Hello, Suki," said Mrs. Paggio. "What did you
do this summer?"

"My grandma visited us," she said, straightening
her sleeves. "She brought me my kimono and my
geta." Suki raised her foot to show the teacher her
wooden clog.

Somewhere in the classroom, someone laughed, but
Suki took a deep breath and continued. "The best thing
was that she took me to a festival. And there were dancing
girls, dressed like me, and they danced like this." She took
a few steps and swayed her arms sideways.

"Look, now she's *dancing*," someone said. But Suki didn't hear.

She hummed the music she remembered hearing at the festival.

She remembered how it felt to dance barefoot in the open air, on fresh-cut grass that tickled her toes.

She tried to picture the other dancers. How they moved forward in the circle with the rhythm of the music. How they stamped their feet, first right, then left, swung their arms, first up, then down. How they stepped back, and back, and back, then clapped.

When Suki couldn't remember the next step, she made it up, just to keep dancing. *One-two, one-two, one-two, stop.*

When she finished, the room seemed very
quiet. Everyone was watching her.

Suki sat down, wondering if she was in trouble.

But Mrs. Paggio said, "That was wonderful, Suki." And she started to clap.

Then, so did Penny.

And after a moment, so did the entire class.

After school, as the three sisters walked home together, Mari and Yumi grumbled about their first day.

"No one even noticed my new sweater," said Mari.

"No one even noticed my cool shoes," said Yumi.

But Suki just smiled.

As she clip-clopped along behind them, Suki pulled out the pale pink handkerchief from her obi and held it up over her head to catch the wind. And in her blue cotton kimono and in her shiny red geta, Suki danced all the way home.